TAKE 1

A MARKET GARDEN TALE

BY L.A. WITT & ALEKSANDR VOINOV

Riptide Publishing
PO Box 6652
Hillsborough, NJ 08844
www.riptidepublishing.com

This is a work of fiction. Names, characters, places, and incidents are either the product of the authors' imagination or are used fictitiously. Any resemblance to actual persons living or dead, business establishments, events, or locales is entirely coincidental.

Take It Off (A Market Garden Tale)
Copyright © 2013 by L.A. Witt and Aleksandr Voinov

Cover Art by L.C. Chase, www.lcchase.com/design.htm
Editor: Rachel Haimowitz
Layout: L.C. Chase, www.lcchase.com/design.htm

All rights reserved. No part of this book may be reproduced or transmitted in any form or by any means, electronic or mechanical, including photocopying, recording, or by any information storage and retrieval system without the written permission of the publisher, and where permitted by law. Reviewers may quote brief passages in a review. To request permission and all other inquiries, contact Riptide Publishing at the mailing address above, at Riptidepublishing.com, or at marketing@riptidepublishing.com.

ISBN: 978-1-62649-003-1

First edition
February, 2013

Also available in ebook:
ISBN: 978-1-62649-002-4

Take It Off
A Market Garden Tale

By L.A. Witt & Aleksandr Voinov

RIPTIDE PUBLISHING

To Aleks, for taking me up on the idea of writing something together, being amazing to work with, and still being along for the ride several books later. Here's to more where that came from! —L.A.

To L.A., for generally rocking my world and making me laugh like a hyena in the office. One day you'll get me fired, but that's okay. —Aleks

T ristan was bored.

At least business had been steadier lately at Market Garden, ever since the Christmas lull had ended. Apparently the wealthy elite had placated all the annual demands for gifts and family time, and could now spare money and evenings for expensive rentboys. Great for the wallet, but as far as Tristan was concerned, the only thing worse than no john was the same john every bloody night. Well, not the exact same guy. Just an endless stream of clones coming through the black curtain in search of a night's entertainment. Every one of them wanted the same thing, and they all grinned and smirked like they were the first mugs ever to ask a rentboy to suck a cock or bend over. Yawn.

"I could use a refill." Jared held up his empty glass. "You?"

Tristan looked into his own glass and realised he was almost to the bottom. "Sure. I'll pick up the next one." The drinks were free, but he and Jared took turns fighting the crowd to the bar for refills.

"Sounds good." Jared slid out of the booth and headed for the bar.

Tristan watched him, and couldn't help grinning. There was a sexy little strut in Jared's step these days. Ever since the two of them had started working together and double-teaming johns, Jared had gained some much-needed confidence, and it showed. God, but he was both cute and mouth-watering, and that gorgeous little arse in those tight leather trousers was icing on the cake. He even flirted shamelessly with Raoul and the other bartenders now.

Johns and rentboys alike glanced at Jared, checking out his lithe body in all that gorgeous, tight leather. As Tristan watched them watch Jared, both pride and a hint of jealousy swelled in his chest.

Look all you want, lads. I get to fuck him.

Tristan shivered at the thought. Even if it was only for the sake of performing for their johns and making a few hundred quid, he enjoyed the hell out of being with Jared. With a body like that and a mouth that talented, who wouldn't? Even if they didn't know Jared was also sweet, funny, smart . . .

Jared came back a moment later, drinks in hand, and slid into the booth beside Tristan.

"Thanks," Tristan said.

"Don't mention it."

Tristan slid his hand over Jared's leather-clad thigh under the table in their shadowy booth. At least things had been more interesting since they'd started working together. Fucking a john while Jared watched, or—even better—fucking Jared while the john watched, that kept his interest. Most of the time, anyway. Lately, even that was getting repetitive.

Or rather, frustrating. They had to concentrate on pleasing their paying clients, and those clients nearly always wanted to get involved in more ways than just sitting back and watching, which meant Tristan never could focus exclusively on Jared. The more they did this, the more he wanted to do exactly that. What he wouldn't have given to get Jared alone for a little while, away from the distraction and interference of the guys who kept their wallets nice and fat. The uptight kid had relaxed a lot recently. He'd been inching out of his shell ever since they'd partnered up, and Tristan wanted to know what else Jared had up his sleeve.

Except the more Jared came into his own, the less interested he seemed in Tristan. Lately, it'd been strictly business for him. A performance he could have put on with any other rentboy. He'd even gone back to taking a lot of johns on his own. As more men turned Jared's head, Tristan desperately wanted to work up the nerve to suggest skipping out of work and spending a little time in his flat, doing what they wanted rather than what someone else wanted them to do. Jared seemed to enjoy working with him, but how would he feel about sleeping with Tristan for free? Or even just hanging out and having a conversation that didn't include keeping an eye on the door for would-be clients? Tristan could've sworn there'd been a little crush going on in the beginning, and now he was kicking himself for not making his move before Jared's interest in him cooled in favour of johns and money.

"You boys look bored." Nick, one of the kinkier rentboys, appeared beside their booth with a characteristic smirk on his thin lips. "Slow night?"

"Night's still young." Tristan sipped his soft drink. "What about you?"

Nick shrugged, the gesture extra flippant in true Nick style. "Just waiting for a worthwhile victim to show up." He shifted his always-predatory gaze towards Jared. "You sure you don't want to play with some of the kinky customers?"

Tristan slid his hand further over Jared's leg.

"I don't know," Jared said. "I'm having a pretty good time with the ones I get."

Another shrug. "Suit yourself. But if you ever change your mind . . ."

"I'll give it some thought." Jared sounded sincere. Genuinely interested, not just being polite.

Nick grinned. Tristan said nothing, just ran his thumb back and forth over the inseam of Jared's trousers. Funny, Jared used to squirm under Tristan's touch, but now it was as routine as flirting with potential clients. Something to entice johns and establish that Jared and Tristan worked together with no implications that they *were* together.

Nick glanced at the door, and straightened. "Oh. Looks like tonight's paycheque just arrived. I'll talk to you guys later." With that, he was gone.

"Think we'll ever get a client like one of his?" Jared asked.

"You never know."

"Could be fun." Jared played with his straw. "Good money, too."

"It could." Jealousy flared in Tristan's chest. He wasn't into the same things Nick was. The bondage, the pain play, it was all fine and good, but it wasn't his thing. He liked the power games, just not the implements and bloodshed. He hadn't thought Jared was into that kind of thing either, but everyone knew Nick made a killing servicing the kinkier johns. There was nothing stopping Jared from partnering up with him and getting in on that action.

How the hell do I tell him I want him for myself?

"Hey." Jared leaned closer, lips brushing Tristan's ear. "You remember that guy who paid us to fool around while he watched? The first time, I mean?"

Tristan shivered and squeezed Jared's leg. "How could I forget?"

"Yeah, well." Jared tilted his head towards the door. "Look who just walked in."

Tristan turned his head.

Well, fuck *me.*

There he was. Suited and booted, looking like he owned the place, flashy gold watch peeking out from the end of an expensively tailored suit.

Rolex. We meet again.

And he was coming right towards them, too.

"Looks like we might be making some money tonight," Jared said with a grin.

Is that opportunity I hear knocking? Tristan ran his hand higher up Jared's leg. "Hope he stopped at the bank on his way here."

Rolex strolled up to their table. He gave Jared a long look, then Tristan. "I was hoping you boys would be here tonight."

"We are." Tristan offered a toothy grin. "And you found us. Now what are you going to do with us?"

Rolex seemed to think on it for a moment, as if thrown off his stride, then grinned. "Oh, I've got a little fantasy in mind."

"How kinky are we talking?" Tristan asked. "The place has specialists for the weirder shit." His teeth snapped shut. Best not to give Rolex—or Jared—any ideas that might subtract Tristan from the night's equation.

Rolex glanced around. "Nothing weird. You guys know I like to watch." He leaned closer, flattening his palms on the table. "And give some orders along the way."

"Orders, eh?" Tristan flashed him a wide grin, and Rolex laughed, clearly picking up the challenge. Tristan reached for his drink. "It's a rematch, then?"

Rolex pushed his tongue against his teeth. "Yeah. In a manner of speaking."

Tristan was intrigued enough that he glanced at Jared, picking up the nod there. It might not be just watching, but by now they'd had enough experience to play basically any john who entered the Garden by ear. Oddly, two against one wasn't fair—even if the other guy called the shots. Totally different to play this game as a team. And they were a bloody good team, especially when paired up with a john as hands-off as Rolex.

"You ready to spend some money?" Tristan asked. *You ready to watch me seduce him for real?*

Rolex didn't flinch. "I think I'm over my sticker shock from the last time."

"Good. Let's go."

Jared slid out of the booth, Tristan hot on his heels, and they walked alongside the john, flanking him no differently from two tarts picked up by the same sugar daddy. It flattered the guys' egos, that was for sure.

Rolex put an arm around Jared, but kept his right hand free to push the curtain aside and open the door. Tristan felt an odd twinge deep in his chest—not because the john seemed more interested in Jared, but because the touch looked almost intimate, and Jared was doing a great job of looking mightily pleased with himself.

All part of the game, Tristan thought. He would have plenty of opportunity to be touched by Jared.

By the john, he quickly corrected himself. Not Jared. The john. The guy with the money.

Tristan shook himself as he followed them out into the night. Had to keep his head in the game. The more he stayed in control, the more money he could squeeze out of this guy's very well-stocked wallet. Not to mention draw things out with Jared.

Head. In the game. Come on.

There were always plenty of luxury cars in front of the Garden, usually with hired drivers, but that stretched Jag immediately drew his attention. Oh, yeah, he remembered that car, or at least one very similar to it. Riding in the back with Jared beside him and the john eyeing them like he thought he stood a chance at being in charge that night. Yeah, right. Tristan didn't give up control. Sure, he took orders, but he took them on *his* terms, and his johns bloody well liked it. Just like Rolex had, and just like he would tonight. And hopefully Jared would too.

The driver held open the door, and the three of them filed in: Jared, then the john, then Tristan.

Before the door had even shut behind them, Rolex caught Tristan off-guard.

Sliding a hand over Jared's leather clad arse, the john said, "Why don't you sit here? With me?"

Being the consummate professional he was, Jared didn't hesitate to let himself be guided not just to Rolex's side of the huge backseat across from Tristan, but right onto the man's lap. Jared's slim, elegant body was compact enough he could arrange himself across the john's legs and avoid hitting his head on the ceiling in the process. He glanced at Tristan, and the saucy gleam in his eyes relaxed Tristan a little. As long as Jared wasn't nervous or uncomfortable, they could play this man's game. At least until it was time for Tristan to play *his* game, and subtly—one kiss, touch, thrust at a time—tell Jared he wanted more than money.

Tristan eased himself onto the seat facing the two of them. As the car pulled away from the curb, he caught himself watching Rolex's hand—gold watch, gold ring, long, slim fingers—sliding from Jared's knee up towards his arse. Tristan forced himself not to fidget or even curl his own fingers on the leather upholstery beside him, searching for some sensation like the one Rolex was no doubt feeling just now—Jared's body heat through slick leather, lean muscles underneath.

"So I'm curious," the john said, eyeing Tristan as he continued stroking Jared's leg. "How did two young men like you wind up working for Market Garden?"

"Likely the same way you got started in your line of work." Tristan ran the toe of his boot up the inside of Rolex's leg, grinning when the john sucked in a breath. "You find a skill you can sell, and you fucking sell it."

"Well." Rolex squirmed a bit under Jared as Tristan's toe neared the inside of his knee. "So you . . . you just showed up with a resume and started working there?"

"Not quite." Jared's hand drifted down and found the laces of Tristan's boot, and he squeezed gently. "You don't just waltz into Market Garden and get a job unless you have . . . experience."

Tristan pressed his foot into Jared's hand. "That, and you don't find Market Garden. Market Garden finds you."

Rolex snickered. "In Soviet Russia, whorehouse finds you?"

Jared snorted. Tristan allowed himself a quiet laugh. "Something like that."

"And how did Market Garden find the two of you?"

Jared's thumb traced the arch of Tristan's foot, the dull contact making Tristan's pulse race in spite of the layer of leather between their skin. "We were both strippers."

"That explains it," Rolex said.

"Explains what?"

Rolex grinned at him. "That confidence oozing out of you. Commanding the stage. And the body." He slid a hand along Jared's lean rump. "Proper pole dancing?"

Tristan nodded, not quite sure what the guy was going for. Complimenting them, or trying to get into their heads? "If you want to see a good pole dancer, we can give you some pointers."

"H-how'd you learn to do that?" Rolex was clearly having a hell of a time keeping his thoughts straight. Tristan couldn't blame him, not with Jared's arse in the flustered man's lap.

"On-the-job training," Tristan said.

"And I did ballet for a while." Jared squirmed just a bit on Rolex's lap while the man's hand explored his torso. Nothing overtly sexual, though the john touching Jared *at all* was surely erotic. He didn't touch him under his clothes, just stroked the side of his body, from the ribs to his hipbone, stroking, caressing, even gripping, long fingers occasionally kneading Jared in a *very* suggestive way.

"Yeah, you're very . . . limber," the john said close to Jared's ear. "I should have guessed you were both dancers."

Tristan made himself look away, and glanced out the window as the car turned a corner. Familiar territory, hotels and expensive shops. Same general neighbourhood as last time, so they were likely headed for the same hotel. Rolex was a creature of habit, then.

He looked at Jared and the john again, and watched Rolex's hand stray up to Jared's chest, fingers splaying to cup his pec through the T-shirt, Jared's nipple hard and visible between his first and second finger. Rolex closed those two fingers, squeezing Jared's nipple hard enough that Jared let out a small gasp.

"Just beautiful." Rolex's gaze shifted towards Tristan. "You of course get him for free, don't you?"

Tristan blinked, thrown out of the role for a moment. Was that the guy's fantasy? Did he want to pretend he was fucking a couple? If that was what rocked the guy's boat, he could play that.

"Maybe I do," he said.

Jared threw him an odd look, confusion furrowing his brow for a split second, and Tristan wondered if he'd overstepped. But Jared recovered quickly. "He gets whatever he wants." Trailing a finger down Rolex's arm, he grinned and added, "Everyone else has to pay for the privilege."

Tristan gulped. What he wouldn't have given . . .

"You boys still dance for each other?" Rolex asked in that husky voice that said he was really getting into this. "Little lap dance once in a while?"

Jared shrugged. "Can't say I've ever danced for him." His gaze slid towards Tristan. "We've never done that, have we?"

This little bit of role-playing was going to be the death of him, Tristan was sure of it. He cleared his throat. "No, we haven't. In fact, I've never seen you dance."

"Never?" Rolex squeezed Jared's arse. "Maybe we should fix that."

Oh God.

"Oh yeah?" Jared arched an eyebrow. "What do you have in mind?" Well, at least one of them had the ballsy confidence tonight. Tristan chastised himself silently, trying to get his mind back on track. This was so not like him.

"I think . . ." Rolex watched his hand sliding down Jared's thigh. "I want to see you dance."

Tristan moistened his lips. "Dance, how?"

"You." Rolex tapped the centre of Jared's chest with a single finger. "On his lap." The finger pivoted towards Tristan.

Jared slowly swept his tongue across his lower lip as he turned his head. "I think we can swing that."

Damn it. Rolex had just changed the rules, hadn't he?

Very well. Tristan could work with that. He could play by the john's rules and still hold the reins.

Tristan cleared his throat again. "It'll cost you."

Rolex laughed dryly. "With as much as the two of you cost me last time, I have no doubt about that." His hand returned to Jared's chest, and slowly slid downwards. "I came prepared, don't worry." He paused, hand resting just above Jared's belt. "How much are we talking?"

Tristan glanced at Jared, and Jared gave him the slight nod that had become their code for "You name the price." Jared still deferred to him on monetary matters, which was fine with Tristan since it kept him in control of the situation. To Rolex, he said, "Hundred quid for the dance."

"That's it?"

Tristan grinned. "That's for the dance only. No clothes coming off."

Rolex started to say something, but then Jared ground against him, likely pressing that stunning arse right against the man's cock. "Holy shit . . ."

"You want anything off?" Tristan forced his voice not to betray how much *he* was getting turned on by this. "Hundred quid. Per piece."

"Per *piece*?" Rolex's eyes widened, then closed when Jared pressed into him again. "Fuck . . ."

"He's only wearing so much," Tristan said. "And it's not the easy-to-remove shit we wore onstage, so he's going to have to work at getting those leather trousers off"—*fucking hell, yes, baby, take them off*—"without breaking his stride."

"And once everything is off?" The john licked his lips. "Then what?"

Tristan shrugged with one shoulder. "Same as before. You want to turn up the heat, you lay down another hundred and we'll talk." *And you can put a stripped-down Jared right into my hot little hands.*

Rolex closed his eyes. He said nothing, but his lips moved, and Tristan was sure they formed another "holy shit."

Jared glanced at Tristan and winked. Tristan returned it, along with a grin. He hoped he'd managed to mask just how much this was exciting him. A night with a john was business as usual, but Jared? Dancing? Stripping? On his lap? Maybe that wasn't the original plan, but Tristan could run with it. He just hoped to God that Rolex had brought enough money to pay for Tristan to fuck the hell out of Jared before the night was over. Or else he might have to beg Jared to let him, and Tristan was *not* one to beg.

"Well, if you want me to dance," Jared said, squirming in the man's lap again, "I'm gonna need some music."

With a hand that wasn't nearly as steady as it had been before, Rolex fished a smartphone out of his pocket. "Here. Hundreds of songs. Use whatever you want."

Jared eyed the screen. "If there isn't anything on here I can dance to, it's going to be another hundred."

Rolex swallowed. "Hell, download more if you want. I don't care. Let's just . . ." He gestured out the window at the hotel, which the car was approaching. "Do this."

Yes. Yes, let's do this.

On the way into the hotel and up the elevator, Jared searched through the john's musical library. "Ooh, you've got Kylie." He flashed a grin at Rolex. "Looks like we're in business."

Rolex snorted. "What gay man doesn't have some Kylie?"

"Well, if you didn't have it already," Jared said, sliding the man's phone into his own back pocket, "you would have had some before too long." He looked at Tristan. "I'm ready for this. How about you?"

Tristan slid an arm around Jared's waist. Looking straight at the john, he whispered in Jared's ear, "I am *so* ready for this." *And then some.*

"Me too," Jared said just as softly. "An hour or two of work, and neither of us has to worry about rent for a while."

Tristan's heart sank a bit, but he tried not to let it show. Rent. Of course.

Rolex opened the hotel room door for them and gestured, not towards the bedroom, but the living room area of the suite. This time, the champagne was already in the bucket. Three glasses. Rolex had been very confident (or hopeful) they'd be there.

Jared walked towards the sideboard with the smartphone dock, then navigated the menu on the phone. Setting up a playlist? Tristan inhaled deeply, trying to think clearly enough to set this up well for the john. Rolex was running the show, he was paying for it, and that meant he had to get off on it, ideally in a blacking-out kind of spectacular way. And preferably in some way, Tristan thought as his gaze slid towards Jared, that wouldn't keep him from pursuing what he wanted tonight.

Rolex settled on the couch, so Tristan found a straight-backed chair slid under a desk in the far corner and pulled that behind himself, positioning it opposite. Rather than facing the john fully, he opted for a three-quarters angle, which would give Rolex the best view of both of them.

"Ever had a lap dance?" the john asked.

"Can't say I have."

"You should come over to the States. I know some spectacular places."

Tristan grinned. "Wall Street?"

"Not where I had in mind, but yes, there too." The john smiled at him and winked. "Champagne to relax?"

"I don't drink on the job."

"I still need to understand how a control freak like you became a rentboy." The john seemed mildly curious. There was no venom or spite in his words.

You know, that's not so strange.

"I'm good at what I do," was all Tristan offered.

"Yes," Rolex said over the top of his glass, "you certainly are."

Jared pulled out another straight-backed chair and set it up a few feet away from Tristan, facing him. Tristan's heart sped up again. Jared was pulling out all the stops, wasn't he? Dancing in an empty chair before dancing on Tristan. Teasing, of course, but maybe that would give Tristan a little time—the length of a song, at least—to plan how he'd take back control and let Jared know, in no uncertain terms, *I want you.*

Keeping the minuscule remote between his fingers, Jared said, "Ready?"

The john nodded and gestured, so Tristan sat down on the chair. Jared regarded him critically, then leaned in and tapped the inside of his knee. Tristan opened his legs. And wider when Jared indicated.

Rolex sipped his champagne, and then put the glass down with a quiet clink. "So the rule is, you're not allowed to touch him. At all." The john smirked. "Isn't that fun?"

Tristan swallowed. "But you get to change the rules if you want to?"

Rolex grinned. "You're smart boys. I like that."

Tristan looked up at Jared. The way Jared grinned back at him made his heart beat even faster. Oh, yes. Jared was already enjoying this. And Tristan hadn't forgotten his own favourite thing about stripping: the sadistic joy of grinding and undulating on a man who had no choice but to sit still and take it.

Sit still and take it, which was exactly what *he* had to do this time. Oh. *Shit.*

Stay in control. Remember the goal tonight. Head in the game. Eye on the prize.

"All right." Jared gestured at the couch cushion beside Rolex. "You can put the money there whenever you pony up another hundred."

Rolex gulped. So did Tristan. Goddamn, but he liked this bold new side of Jared. Though he'd been a little shy and uncertain when he'd come to Market Garden, he must've been one hell of a confident dancer, and that must've been what'd caught Frank's eye when he'd recruited him. Whatever the case, Tristan had only seen it for a few minutes, hadn't even seen him dance yet, and he loved it already.

Obediently, Rolex put a hundred quid on the cushion beside him. "There. Ready when you are."

"Good." Jared clicked the remote and then set it aside. As the music started up—some typical upbeat dance song—Jared's body started moving like it was hard-wired into the sound system. One step at a time, he strode towards Tristan, eyes locked on his, hands on his hips as they moved in perfect time with the music. He stopped just short of Tristan's knee, their legs almost touching, but not.

Tristan's eyes flicked past him, towards the other chair. Against his will, his mind showed him Jared's slim, sexy body writhing on and bending over that chair. Oh fuck. He swallowed hard and looked up at Jared again.

Skip the second chair and dance on me. Please.

Jared grinned. Winked. He trailed a finger down the centre of his own chest, and Tristan couldn't help watching it follow a straight path down the tight black T-shirt, across Jared's abs, and to his belt buckle. There, it stopped, but Tristan's eyes kept going. Right to the pronounced bulge beneath Jared's trousers.

He looked up at Jared's face again. Jared bit his lip, then grinned, just the way Tristan had often done to the men he'd teased to within an inch of their lives.

You're going to kill me tonight. You know that, right?

As if reading Tristan's mind, Jared licked his lips, winked again, and then turned around. One provocative, choreographed step at a time, equal parts stripper and classically trained dancer, Jared sauntered towards that other chair. The empty chair. The one Tristan wasn't sitting in, fuck it.

Tristan curled his fingers around the edges of the seat on either side of him, no doubt turning his knuckles white. He inhaled deeply and watched, mesmerized, as Jared made a slow, slinking gesture of leaning over the other chair. He rested a hand on the back of it, then pulled one knee up onto the seat, and the way the leather stretched tight across his arse made Tristan's breath catch. The little snap of his hips to one side, then the other, didn't help at all.

Tristan made himself breathe slowly and deeply. Eye on the prize, indeed.

"Are you—" The john's voice startled Tristan. He'd all but forgotten there was someone else in the room. "Are you going to dance over there? Or on him?"

Jared turned around, lowering himself onto the hard chair and straddling it. "You telling the dancer how to dance?"

Both Rolex and Tristan watched Jared slide a hand down his abs on onto the front of his trousers, and Tristan had no idea which of the two of them made that helpless "oh fuck" whimper as Jared squeezed his own erection through the leather.

"I want . . . I want to see you . . ." The john swore under his breath. "I want to see you on him."

"Do you?" Jared slid his gaze towards Rolex. "Make me."

Tristan didn't know where this sassy side of Jared was coming from, but Jesus fuck, it was hot.

With shaking hands, Rolex freed a couple notes from his wallet and added it to the one already lying on the cushion. "There." He nodded sharply towards Tristan. "On him. Now."

Jared grinned. "I do love it when you ask nicely." He took his sweet time rising from the chair, and was in absolutely no hurry to get to the other. When he made it to Tristan, he stood with both legs between Tristan's knees and slid his hands over Tristan's shoulders. He leaned down, and his breath was hot on Tristan's neck as he whispered, "Enjoying this?"

"You're a motherfucking tease," Tristan said before he could stop himself. *I want you so bad.*

"Of course I am." Jared drew back. "Would you really want me any other way right now?"

Tristan's mouth went dry. He couldn't think anything except that this was likely payback for every time he'd fucked Jared and made him beg for it to score more money. Shit, it was nothing personal. But apologising for something that had put a lot of cash in their pockets and been tremendous fun would have been dishonest. He wasn't sorry, and Jared had never protested.

Though, it dawned on him now, that didn't mean Jared hadn't been plotting revenge. Fuck.

A small flick from Jared's finger changed the music, and now it was much slower, Kylie's singing sensuous and breathy. Jared turned in front of Tristan, bent over a bit, curved his spine, nearly pushing his arse against Tristan's chest. Before Tristan had managed to break the tension with so much as a breath, Jared brought his knees together and kept his hands on Tristan's thighs as his hips swayed from side to side, long legs bending and straightening as the circles became wider, looser. All the moves of a female lap dancer, as far as Tristan was familiar with them, but Jared pulled them off in a way that was sexy and masculine and uniquely *him.*

Straightening, Jared turned around, the one-eighty executed with all the grace of a perfect pirouette. His hands slipped under his T-shirt, pushing it up to flash his toned abs, then slid again over his groin, left and right of his bulge, thumbs extended, framing his erection in a triangle, hip movements slow and thrusting as if fucking into and through his fingers.

"Take off the shirt," the john said, and immediately put the cash down.

Jared didn't hesitate, though he also didn't rush. He condensed his rhythmic movements somehow, making them less overt, small and sensuous. His hands slid up under his shirt, rucking it up as if by accident, revealing his abs one muscle at a time, his flat belly button, the gentle curve of his pecs. Then in a single, smooth motion, he pulled off the T-shirt, his muscles sliding under his pale skin as he kept dancing. The T-shirt dropped to the floor between his feet. He turned around, folded his upper body down, legs straight and opened, arse pushed out as he retrieved his shirt. As he stood, he swept the shirt over his torso as if he were drenched in sweat. He wasn't, though. He wasn't even really worked up. Unlike Tristan, who already had perspiration cooling the back of his neck beneath the ends of his hair. From the corner of his eye, he saw Rolex wipe a hand across his brow.

Jared, still calm and cool, tossed the wadded up shirt in Rolex's lap. Some guys would've picked it up and pressed it to their faces, breathing in deeply. Tristan had no idea if Rolex did that or not. His eyes were locked on Jared's sinewy body, the way he moved, the way he touched his own torso, hips, legs. Every time Jared's hand ran over his own erection, Tristan swore his got even harder. All the times he'd teased and fucked Jared before, he'd always been turned on as hell, but never like this. Never to the point he could barely think, and probably wouldn't be able to string together a coherent sentence if someone asked him to.

"Get—" Rolex cleared his throat. "The boots. Take them off."

"That'll cost you." Jared rose and leaned back against Tristan. His arse ground against Tristan's hard cock, and his bare torso was hot through Tristan's T-shirt. "A hundred per boot."

At least one of them still had the presence of mind to keep after the money. Of course Jared did. This was business for him. All business. As it should have been, even if Tristan held out hope for more.

"Gonna go broke with you two." Rolex pulled out another hundred, but he didn't put it down yet. "*One* hundred for both boots."

Tristan bit his lip, staring at Jared's back and silently begging him to agree to it.

"Fine." Jared writhed a little harder against Tristan. "Put it down, and the boots come off."

Please put it down. Please put it down. Fuck, dude, seriously, put it the fuck—

Rolex put the money on the cushion.

Jared didn't get up. Oh, no, that would've been entirely too easy. He leaned down, arse still pressed firmly against Tristan's erection. Tristan's mouth watered as he watched him, their bodies locked together in a crude pantomime of the times they'd been stripped down to nothing except a condom and Tristan had thrust into Jared while Jared made helpless noises and cursed and fell apart.

Except Tristan was still dressed. And there was no thrusting. Because he couldn't move. At all.

As Jared unlaced his boots, the muscles in his back, arms, and shoulders moved subtly, and those hypnotic movements happened in time with the music. Everything the man did was in perfect time. Perfectly rhythmic. Perfectly calculated. And absolute torture.

Jared sat up again, reached back, and held onto Tristan's hips as he pressed his back against Tristan's chest. He lifted both feet up, the laces dangling from his boots, and toed them off. Then his socks. All the while pressing against, rubbing against, *grinding* against Tristan.

Hands still on Tristan's thighs, Jared lifted himself up a little. Tristan relaxed somewhat, thinking he'd just been granted some breathing room, but Jared had other plans. Room to breathe? No. Room to *move*. Keeping his palms flat on Tristan's legs, Jared continued to dance on him, kept lifting up, then leaning back, then lifting up again, sometimes touching and sometimes just making Tristan watch.

"More." Rolex panted. "More. Take . . . take off the belt."

"With pleasure."

Oh shit. Jared didn't even demand more money, and that grin in his voice said Tristan hadn't even begun to know what "torture" really meant.

Jared got up and turned around. He put one leg over Tristan's. Then the other. Straddling him. Tristan had the most tantalizing view of nearly everything Jared had to offer: that gorgeous chest, those amazing abs, not to mention that very pronounced erection all wrapped up in slick black leather.

Their eyes met. Jared's were hot with lust, and there it was, that gleam of raw desire Tristan had seen the first time. Tristan's heart skipped. He very nearly reached for Jared's face to draw him into a kiss, but then Jared grinned and it was back to strictly business.

Jared leaned back. Way back. He must've had his ankles hooked around the legs of the chair. Something. Somehow, he balanced perfectly, his torso almost horizontal. His abs were taut with the exertion of holding himself like that, his legs pressing hard against Tristan's lap, and Tristan couldn't fucking breathe.

Rolex cleared his throat. "The belt. Take it off."

"Don't rush me." Jared looked right at Tristan. "There's a method to my madness." His hands materialized on Tristan's calves, and Tristan's heart pounded as Jared ran them up. Down. Up again. In a smooth, fluid motion, they went from Tristan's legs to his own hips, drawing a curving path over his cock—*yeah, Tristan, you see how hard I am*—before coming back up to his belt buckle. His abs were quivering now, his leg muscles rock hard over the tops of Tristan's thighs, and the cords in his neck stood out slightly as he continued to hold himself in that perfectly balanced position.

He unbuckled his belt, then tugged it free, leather hissing over leather as it slid out of the loops. Without breaking eye contact with Tristan, he dropped his belt, and then pulled himself up using only his legs and his toned abs. He wrapped those legs around Tristan and the back of the chair, pressing their clothed cocks together, and then kissed Tristan hard.

"*I'm not usually a kisser,*" Tristan had said to Jared a while back. "*But the johns like it. A lot.*"

"*Do they?*" Jared had grinned, and hadn't hesitated to kiss since then.

For the johns. Because the johns liked it. Jared was doing this for Rolex. Just for the john. But Tristan indulged anyway, tangling his tongue with Jared's and kissing him like he meant it, because fuck it, he did. As deeply, passionately, intimately as he could without breaking the rules and taking his hands off the chair.

"That is fucking amazing," Rolex breathed. "Holy shit."

My sentiments exactly.

Jared broke the kiss. For a split second, he looked breathless and flustered, and it was sweet, shy Jared holding Tristan's gaze. Then his eyes narrowed as he swept his tongue across his lips. "Only one thing left. Just the trousers." His grin made Tristan's heart pound even harder, especially when he added, "Better make it count."

Tristan tried so hard to clear his head, just enough to regain control of the money negotiations, because he needed that one last bit of control over something. Though, fucking hell, this performance alone was worth being so precariously close to falling apart.

Tristan turned his head towards the john, who leaned forwards on the couch. He'd taken off his jacket, his cufflinks too, rolled up his fine white sleeves, and his lower arms showed the tension, his muscles and sinews playing as he balled his fists and loosened them again. Just what kind of kick did a guy get out of watching alone? Seemed like a waste when he could have fucked them both, or joined them.

Whatever.

Jared got up, then put a hand on Tristan's shoulder and walked around him, running his fingers over Tristan's chest, down his pecs, making sure he was rubbing against his nipples. He slid his hands further down until they framed Tristan's cock in his trousers—all for the john's viewing pleasure, and yeah, to drive Tristan just that little bit more insane as the leather tightened over his erection. One hand continued down and cupped his balls.

"You are so hot when you're frustrated," Jared whispered, so softly only Tristan could have heard. Which meant that was just for him, not Rolex. Tristan's stomach fluttered, but before he could respond, Jared said to the john, "I'm down to trousers and nothing else." His lips brushed Tristan's cheek. "What about him?"

The john laughed dryly. "He's fine."

Oh, you bastard. Tristan bit back a groan when Jared slid back up, palm running over his cock, giving him some sweet pressure, but it didn't last very long.

Jared chuckled. "I tried."

Tristan was nearly shaking on his chair. He tightened his hands around the seat and thought he heard it creak a little. Jared came back around, never breaking the touch, then put both hands on Tristan's thighs. He slid down onto his knees, bringing his face very close to the leather seam of Tristan's trousers, like he was about to give him a blowjob.

"I want—" The john moved forward. "Take him out of his trousers. Show me his cock."

Jared lifted his head just enough to look the john in the eye. "Just show you? Or should I touch him?"

"Yeah. Both." Without missing a beat, the john put more money down.

This was as far removed from a normal lap dance as it could be, but Tristan was glad some of that pressure would ease now. His cock was trying already to punch through the leather, and that part wasn't fun anymore. Jared opened Tristan's fly, still mimicking a blowjob as he pulled the zipper down and folded the leather back, then pulled Tristan's briefs down far enough to bare his cock. He pushed the briefs down under Tristan's balls, exposing him to anything Jared wanted to do to him.

The music continued. Jared's snake-like movements turned into something different as the tip of his tongue slid all the way from the root of Tristan's cock to the tip. This . . . this was getting out of hand extremely fast, and Tristan definitely felt the chair creak as he tensed and forced himself to stay still and quiet.

Didn't I have a plan tonight? Wasn't I going to . . . didn't I . . . there was . . .

Jared looked up at him, his face flushed a bit, his eyes gleaming with mischief and power. It said *Got you*, and *Payback*, and *What now, Tristan?*

Tristan shook his head but forced a grin.

A grin that evaporated the second Jared took every inch of Tristan's cock into his mouth. Tristan gasped. Shuddered. He pulled in a breath and held it, his entire body rigid as he fought to stay in something like control. Jared's head bobbed over Tristan, moving in time with the music, and his hand slid up the side of Tristan's thigh, almost to his arse, and then his fingers pressed in slightly. Dug in. He drew his hand back, fingers squeaking across the leather and making Tristan even crazier because he wanted Jared's hand on his skin. Touching him. Just like Jared's mouth was, his lips and tongue teasing painfully sensitive flesh while his fingers were kept at bay by thin leather.

"Don't you fucking come yet," Rolex growled.

Tristan gritted his teeth. The explicit denial of his orgasm made it that much harder to hold back.

Wait. Shouldn't I be telling him I won't come until he pays? What the hell is going on tonight?

Something rustled. More money. Oh fuck, they were turning up the heat again.

"Trousers off."

Jared slowly lifted off Tristan's cock, pausing to swirl his tongue around the tip once before he looked at Rolex. "Whose? His or mine?"

Rolex swallowed. "Yours."

Jared waited for the money to join the growing stack. Then he looked up at Tristan. "I think that can be arranged, don't you?"

Tristan moistened his lips. "I think so. Yes." *Please, please take them off.*

Jared leaned in and dropped a light kiss on Tristan's mouth. Before Tristan could make sense of that or even try to return the kiss, Jared stood. He stayed very close, his groin inches from Tristan's mouth. And, of course, his hips moved. God, they *moved*. Tristan didn't even know if they were in synch with the music anymore. He couldn't even hear the music anymore. He only knew that Jared, with his swivelling and undulating punctuated by the occasional hip snap to one side or the other, drove him insane. He wanted nothing more than to grab those hips, hold on tight, and drive himself into Jared again and again until Jared came and Tristan relieved this ache. The thought of getting Jared off—God, the sounds he made when he came—only made things worse, and Tristan held the sides of the chair so tight he thought he was going to snap off a piece of the wood.

Just as Jared had done everything else tonight, he made a deliberate, calculated display of unbuttoning and unzipping his trousers. Tristan's jaw ached as he ground his teeth, watching the zipper separate one tooth at a time. Beneath it, Jared's erection strained against the leather, just waiting to be freed, and Tristan's mouth watered. He swore he could already hear the john telling him to suck that cock, and he was more than willing to obey whether or not there was money involved.

Tight leather trousers didn't come off easily or smoothly, but damn if Jared hadn't gotten that memo. He slid his hands under the waistband, hooked his thumbs over it, and pushed downwards, using the never-ending motions of his hips to work himself out of the trousers. With a mind-blowing shimmy, he freed his thick erection, and Tristan thought he heard himself whisper "Bloody hell" as Jared continued to peel the leather off his toned legs.

Movement beside him caught Tristan's attention, and he stole a glance at Rolex. The john was slowly stroking his groin through his trousers as he watched, slack-jawed. His eyes flicked towards Tristan's, narrowed by some unspoken thought, and Tristan was sure he saw a challenge there.

No way I'm coming before you do.

You're losing it, aren't you?

Tristan smirked. *Make me.*

He turned back to Jared just in time to see him step out of his last stitch of clothing. It was impossible to say if Jared stopped to let Tristan take in the sight, or if time itself had stopped, but Tristan just stared at him. Head to toe, taking in every inch of lean, powerful muscles, narrow hips, sculpted abs with only the thinnest treasure trail leading from his navel to his cock, which he was stroking with one fine hand.

Tristan looked up at his face. Jared's skin was flushed, and . . . that grin. Fuck. He was totally in control right now, and he *knew* it. Tristan didn't have a submissive bone in his body, but if Jared was like this when he was on top, there wasn't much Tristan wouldn't do if Jared snapped his fingers and demanded it.

Holy fuck, what is wrong with me?

Jared took a step forwards, and time lurched back into motion. He put a bare knee on the chair in front of Tristan, his thigh nearly touching Tristan's exposed balls, close enough to share some body heat, and then put his hands on the back of the chair as he leaned in close. "Like what you see?"

Tristan nodded mutely, just like a mesmerised, turned on, nearly insane strip club patron.

Jared's grin turned even more devilish. Still looking right at Tristan, he said, "You know, he could fuck me like this if you coughed up another, say, two hundred?"

Tristan almost choked, and it wasn't because of the price.

"I do love the way you think," Rolex said. "Here."

Jared turned, and Rolex tossed a condom to him. Jared caught it. Then came the small bottle of lube. "I'll put this on him." Jared tore the condom wrapper with his teeth. "You get the money out."

"On it, don't worry," Rolex murmured. "And you"—he looked up from thumbing through the cash and met Tristan's eyes—"no coming 'til I pay for that, right?"

Tristan swallowed. "Right."

"That seems kind of cruel, don't you think?" Jared wrapped his fingers around Tristan's cock and started rolling on the condom. "I *like* it."

Groaning, Tristan closed his eyes and let his head fall back. A dry laugh reminded him of the unspoken power game with the john, of his own refusal to let someone see him lose control, and he forced himself to recover. He raised his head and blinked his eyes into focus. Deep breath. In control. *I've got this.*

That was, until Jared opened the bottle of lube and poured some into his hand.

Oh fuck.

Their eyes met as Jared ran his lubed hand up and down Tristan's erection. Tristan searched his expression, silently begging for some sign there was more going on here than a transaction. Even the faintest flicker of genuine lust. Something.

Jared grinned, but before Tristan could decide what that meant, Jared turned around again. He pushed his arse out, running his fingers into and along his own crack, teasing Tristan with the view and those rolling hip movements that wouldn't have been out of place on a deliciously slutty harem boy.

Then he turned around again and stepped on the chair between Tristan's legs, sliding down into a crouch, hands on Tristan's shoulders to steady himself, though his balance and poise were perfect. He sat nearly back on his heels, his cock rubbing against Tristan's for the first time in *God way too long.*

But he pushed his arse out towards the john, one hand reaching back. He sucked in a sharp breath, probably as he breached himself with his fingers, and Tristan wished he could see that, even if it cost him his last bit of sanity. Jared moistened his lips, closed his eyes, and pushed further back as he played with his arsehole in front of the john. Tristan was breathless, needed to remind himself that, according to the rules, he wasn't allowed to touch. Jared was running this, and just how well he did it shocked Tristan to the core. Jared was cute and sweet, a twink who could look so innocent and fresh, but this wicked sex kitten persona really rattled Tristan. Rattled him and threw him off his game. The more Tristan saw of this side of Jared, the harder it was to focus on conveying how much he wanted *all* sides of him.

"How . . . how's this gonna work?" he whispered.

"Don't worry about it, honey." Jared grinned at him. "Just remember, the *dancer* does the pole dance. The pole stays still."

Oh. Hell. Fucking. Hell.

"I'll strangle you," Tristan mouthed.

"Hot." Jared grinned at him, straightening up already, sliding his leg back before doing another one of those sharp turns.

Scorching. Tristan was sure his skin would turn to ash, he was so hot now, and he had no way to react, move, or do as much as fidget. Not when Jared shook his arse at him again before lowering himself onto Tristan's groin—or nearly. He reached back, took Tristan's cock and, slowly, oh so slowly, hips still moving, undulated and teased Tristan head with every near-brush and bit of pressure.

Just when Tristan thought he could take no more, Jared pushed back, both their legs open wide so the john had a perfect view of Jared impaling himself.

It was mind-bending, the pressure, the heat, and just knowing he was inside *Jared*, and still Jared moved, grinding, sliding, up and down, completely in control of every motion. Tristan gasped and moaned, too fucking close to losing it, and it only got worse when Jared took Tristan's hands—damn near wrenched them off the seat of the chair—and put them on his naked torso. "Make sweet love to me, baby," Jared whispered, rolling his hips just *so*.

Tristan was in no state to laugh at the cheesy line. Performance. They were giving the john what he wanted, so he ran his fingers, his palms along that slinking body on top of his, all the way down to Jared's cock, hard and gorgeous.

"Don't touch him," the john said.

Shit. Please? "But he—"

"You heard him." Jared took Tristan's wrists and lifted his hands away. Tristan whimpered softly as he grabbed onto the chair again, fingers and palms still warm from Jared's hot skin. He bit his lip, dug his teeth in *hard*, gripping the chair like it could somehow keep him from losing his already tenuous grasp on control.

"*Fuck.*" He closed his eyes. "Oh fuck . . ."

"My, my, he wears 'losing it' well, doesn't he?" Rolex taunted.

"He does." Jared reached back and held onto Tristan's hips as he kept riding him in time with the music still playing somewhere in the background. "Don't you, darling?"

Tristan didn't care. He didn't care at all. Let them tease him, because he couldn't think past his impending orgasm and this taut, gorgeous body moving up and down on his cock—*holy* fuck, *Jared*—and he was *this close* to calling time on their game and just fucking the hell out of Jared.

"Faster," Rolex said, almost whispering. "Do it faster."

"With pleasure," Jared purred, and obeyed.

Tristan shut his eyes tighter and held his breath. That didn't help. His head just got lighter, and his orgasm just got closer, and he couldn't remember ever being inside someone who moved like that, as if Jared wasn't about to stop performing his lap dance just because he was getting fucked.

Getting fucked? Hardly. Tristan may have been the one with the condom on, but Jared was in control. Jared was on top. Jared was fucking him. And Tristan was falling apart. No matter how much he held back, the only thing he had a grip on was this bloody chair, and even that wasn't going to last long with the way his hands were sweating.

Movement beside him brought him out of his thoughts. He had just enough time to realize the john wasn't on the couch anymore before a warm hand touched his shoulder. Tristan sucked in a breath. Rolex's hand drifted from Tristan's shoulder to his neck, then up to his face.

"You look like you could use something to keep your mouth busy," the john growled in his ear, and Tristan didn't resist at all as the man slid two fingers into his mouth. Hot, salty skin pressed against his tongue. He closed his eyes again, groaning softly, and sucked Rolex's fingers.

"I should charge you for that," Jared said, and he was out of breath. His voice was shaky, just like it always was when Tristan pushed him right to the brink. Tristan couldn't even grit his teeth, not with those fingers in his mouth, and he groaned again, this time with both frustration and arousal.

"He really knows how to dance, doesn't he?" Rolex whispered.

Before he could tell himself not to fall for it, Tristan opened his eyes, and now he was both watching and feeling Jared rising and falling on Tristan's cock while turning his hips and shoulders. Still dancing. God, he was *still dancing*.

Jared's head fell back. Tristan caught a glimpse of his face in profile, and Jared's lips were pressed together, his brow furrowed. So close. *So* close.

Fuck. To hell with it.

Tristan let go of the seat. He grabbed Rolex's wrist and pulled his fingers from his mouth. Then he grabbed onto Jared's hips and, as much as the position allowed, thrust up into him.

Jared moaned. His body went almost completely slack for a second, but he recovered, and he started to move with Tristan instead of the music.

So what if he'd lost control? So what if he'd lost whatever game they were playing? He couldn't help it. He wanted Jared, needed Jared, had to have Jared, and didn't give a damn about anything else.

"Oh shit," he breathed, and shut his eyes tight. He gritted his teeth, forced himself into Jared, and came so bloody hard, he had to—ironically—grab onto the chair again to keep from collapsing.

He heard husky laughter, turned on and amused, and the john's hand patted his cheek just a bit too hard. "Doesn't seem right to let the disobedient one come and the good boy gets nothing."

"Hardly . . . uh. Nothing." Jared looked back over his shoulder at the john.

The john reached down, steadied himself with one hand on the back of the chair, and then took Jared's hand and wrapped it around his cock, moving. Jared moaned, movements speeding up as the john made him bring himself closer to climax.

Jared got more frantic, less controlled, and just as he was tightening around Tristan's still-hard and hypersensitive cock, he pulled the john down by the neck and kissed him. It was an open-mouthed, hot, grateful kiss that tightened Tristan's balls, and not just with arousal. Jealousy flared in his chest as the john kissed Jared back, stroking him faster and then, when Jared tightened more and came, every muscle in his body taut, stroking him through it.

The john broke the kiss. "That was beautiful." He stepped back, and Tristan saw blotches of semen on his white shirt, making it translucent in places above the massive tent in his hip-hugging tailored trousers.

Then he smirked. "Ooh. It seems I didn't pay for those orgasms." Clicking his tongue, he shook his head. "Such a *shame*."

Tristan felt so bloody good he didn't even care.

Apparently Jared didn't either. He slid off Tristan, turned around, and kissed him, gentle and heartfelt. Real. It was *real*. They were both still out of breath, but Tristan didn't need air badly enough to hurry this kiss, and he let Jared take the lead. Jared teased his lips apart, exploring Tristan's mouth like he was in charge, and they had all the time in the world, and they didn't have a turned on, paying client standing next to them.

"Jesus, that's hot." Rolex stroked Tristan's hair while Tristan and Jared lazily made out. *This isn't for you.* "I could watch you two do that all night."

"I could do it all night," Jared murmured as he drew back from Tristan's lips. He looked up at Rolex. "But we're not done with you yet." He reached for Rolex's waistband, hooked a finger in it, and pulled the man closer. "We should take care of that." Glancing at Tristan and grinning, he added, "Shouldn't we?"

Tristan narrowed his eyes and looked up at Rolex. "For a small fee, yes."

Rolex gulped. "H-how much?"

"Two hundred."

Rolex didn't even blink. Without a word or a second's hesitation, he went to the couch, and Tristan and Jared exchanged grins as the john pulled out some more money. Jared rose up off Tristan's cock, but stayed in his lap. Tristan wrapped one arm around him, grateful just to be able to finally touch his skin, which was damp with perspiration, still almost feverishly hot beneath Tristan's palm.

Once the cash was added to the pile, Rolex returned and stood right beside them. "Now. Where were we?"

"Getting you off, if I recall." Jared reached for Rolex's trousers.

"One of these days," the john said, slurring a little as Jared drew down his zipper, "I'm going to pay for an entire night with the two of you. So I can—" He cut himself off with a throaty groan as Jared stroked him. "So I can fuck you. Both of you."

Tristan shivered. So did Jared.

"Better cash out your retirement fund." Jared looked up as he leaned towards Rolex's exposed cock. "We don't come cheap."

There may have been a snarky retort on the tip of Rolex's tongue, or even Tristan's, but no one said a word as Jared took the john's cock into his mouth just like he had Tristan's earlier. Tristan watched him for a moment, mesmerised, but then joined in, running his lips and tongue up and down the thick shaft as Jared teased the head.

Rolex moaned. His fingers were in Tristan's hair, alternately petting and grasping. Maybe he had a hand in Jared's hair too, but Tristan didn't take the time to look. The john's hips were nowhere near as controlled or rhythmic as Jared's had been. They moved with more of a jerky, frantic need to thrust. Into someone's mouth, into someone's arse, it didn't matter; he just needed to thrust into *something*.

Jared and Tristan teased him together, their lips and tongues brushing as they sucked the man's cock, and then Rolex moaned and tightened his grip on Tristan's hair, pulling his head back. He must have done the same to Jared because they were both suddenly no longer touching Rolex's cock, and just like he had the first time, Rolex took over, jerking himself off until he came on their necks and chests.

He took a few wobbly steps back, and then dropped onto the couch, disturbing the pile of money. After a moment, he pushed himself onto his feet. "I'm gonna . . . go clean up. Be right back." He disappeared into the bedroom, presumably going into the bathroom.

While the john was gone, Jared eased off Tristan's lap, but caught himself with a hand on Tristan's shoulders when his legs tried to shake out from under him.

"You okay?" Tristan asked.

Jared nodded. "Yeah. Yeah, I'm good." He wiped his brow with one hand, and then grinned at Tristan as he stood. "You?"

"Oh, I'm fine." Tristan returned the grin. He rose, got rid of the condom and, as he zipped up his trousers, said, "You're evil. Just so you know."

Jared winked. "Turnabout's fair play."

"So it is. Maybe we—" Tristan hesitated, his pulse skyrocketing.

"Hmm?" Jared leaned down to pick up his clothes. "Maybe we what?"

Tristan glanced towards the bedroom where the john had gone. Then, lowering his voice and hoping he wasn't about to make an arse of himself, he said, "Maybe we should do this again. Without the money."

Jared arched an eyebrow. "What do you mean?"

Tristan swallowed. "I mean . . . not professionally. No"—he nodded towards the bedroom—"company." And fuck it, he couldn't say this without a shaky voice. He could fuck and be fucked and blow a john's mind, but suggesting they move beyond the money, that felt like it took an extra pair of balls.

Jared's eyebrows pulled together.

Please don't be offended. Or shocked. Or laugh at me.

"You mean that?" Jared still looked confused, but there was something else underneath. He brightened—nearly started to beam—and then tamped down on it. "Like, I don't know. Just having sex? Both of us?"

"Yeah." Tristan sighed. "You've been blowing my mind for weeks now. I . . . start to find the *clients* distracting."

Jared glanced at the bathroom. "Dunno, I like that one." He grinned then and looked deep into Tristan's eyes. "Well, technically it would be practice, right?"

Neither Tristan nor Jared had boyfriends—he knew that much about Jared, at least, and had mentioned his own status in the past, but hadn't thought much about it. Not that it would matter, not with his job. "Technically. Maybe not *actually*."

"Dress rehearsal minus dress." Jared put a finger on Tristan's lips, then kissed him again. "I'm game."

Tristan refused to let it show, but weeks' worth of tension melted out of his neck and back. He couldn't ask for more than a step in the right direction. Maybe they wouldn't go much further than this, maybe they would, but after being so certain Jared had lost interest in him, Tristan didn't complain. He was more than happy to cling to this new glimmer of hope that something *might* happen. Something *could* happen.

"You okay with that?" Jared asked.

Tristan nodded. "Yeah. Taking it step by step. My brain needs to reboot. I'm not . . ." *Not yet completely clear.* Yet something gnawed on him, something that wanted more, wanted sweeping off its feet and declarations and weird little cheesy lines like the one Jared had fed him for the john's benefit. "I'm good."

"I know you are." Jared winked. Then he touched Tristan's face and started to lean in for another kiss, but hesitated. "Think the boss will mind if we take the rest of the night off?"

"Not with that stack of cash, he won't."

"Good." This time, Jared did kiss him, and it was another gentle, lazy kiss. "I need to sleep after all this." As he pulled back and started to unravel his shirt so he could put it on, he added, "I probably won't be able to move tomorrow."

"After the way you were dancing?" Tristan shivered. "I'm not surprised."

Jared started to speak, but Rolex strolled back into the room right then.

"Well, as always, you boys were well worth the money." He picked up the notes and handed them to Jared. He kissed Jared lightly, then Tristan. "I'll probably sleep the whole flight back to the States tomorrow."

"So soon?" Tristan grinned. "You know where to find us if you come back."

"Indeed I do."

Jared finished getting dressed, and after a little more banter, they left Rolex to his hotel room. On the way down the hall, Tristan put his arm around Jared's waist just like he had the first night they'd come here with this john.

"We're off tomorrow night," he said.

"We are." Jared put his arm around Tristan's waist too. "But that doesn't mean we have to wait until our next work night to see each other." He glanced up at Tristan. "Does it?"

Tristan's pulse jumped. "No, it doesn't."

But do you want *to wait until our next work night?*

Jared pressed the button for the elevator. "Do you have my mobile number?"

Tristan shook his head.

"I'll give it to you before we leave the Garden." Jared grinned as they stepped onto the lift. "Call me?"

"Absolutely."

Funny, Tristan thought as the doors closed behind them, the one time he let go of control, he got exactly what he wanted.

Maybe I should try that more often.

Acknowledgments

Many thanks to our editor Rachel, and our Britcheckers Gitte, Alex, and Sue, who worked through a weekend to get this ready in time. Thank you! All British English mistakes are Aleks's fault.

Other Market Garden Tales by L.A. Witt & Aleksandr Voinov

Quid Pro Quo
If It Flies (Coming Soon)
If It Fornicates (Coming Soon)

Also by Aleksandr Voinov

Skybound
Incursion
Gold Digger
Country Mouse, with Amy Lane
City Mouse, with Amy Lane (Coming Soon)
Dark Soul Vols. 1–5
Break and Enter, with Rachel Haimowitz
Counterpunch
Scorpion (re-issue with Riptide Publishing, Coming Soon)
Dark Edge of Honor, with Rhi Etzweiler
The Lion of Kent, with Kate Cotoner
Unhinge the Universe, wtih L.A. Witt (Coming Soon)

For a full list, go to www.aleksandrvoinov.com/bookshelf.html

Also by L.A. Witt

The Closer You Get
Conduct Unbecoming
Where There's Smoke
A Chip in His Shoulder
O Come All Ye Kinky
From Out in the Cold
Something New Under the Sun
Covet Thy Neighbor (Coming Soon)
Unhinge the Universe, with Aleksandr Voinov (Coming Soon)

For a full list, please visit www.loriawitt.com

About the Authors

Aleksandr Voinov is an emigrant German author living near London, where he is one of the unsung heroes in the financial services sector. His genres range from horror, science fiction, cyberpunk, and fantasy to contemporary, thriller, and historical erotic gay novels.

In his spare time, he goes weightlifting, explores historical sites, and meets other writers. He singlehandedly sustains three London bookstores with his ever-changing research projects. His current interests include special forces operations during World War II, pre-industrial warfare, European magical traditions, and how to destroy the world and plunge it into a nuclear winter without having the benefit of nuclear weapons.

Visit Aleksandr's website at www.aleksandrvoinov.com, his blog at www.aleksandrvoinov.blogspot.com, and follow him on Twitter, where he tweets as @aleksandrvoinov.

L.A. Witt is an abnormal M/M romance writer currently living in the glamorous and ultra-futuristic metropolis of Omaha, Nebraska, with her husband, two cats, and a disembodied penguin brain that communicates with her telepathically. In addition to writing smut and disturbing the locals, L.A. is said to be working with the U.S. government to perfect a genetic modification that will allow humans to survive indefinitely on Corn Pops and beef jerky. This is all a cover, though, as her primary leisure activity is hunting down her arch nemesis, erotica author Lauren Gallagher, who is also said to be lurking somewhere in Omaha. L.A. can be found at www.loriawitt.com, as well as exchanging irreverent tweets with Aleks as @GallagherWitt.

Enjoy this book?
Find more steamy shorts at
RiptidePublishing.com!

*Are you willing to put yourself
in our hands?*

www.riptidepublishing.com/titles/
surprises-romeo-club-1
ISBN: 978-1-937551-08-7

*Sometimes the earth really
does move.*

www.riptidepublishing.com/titles/
foreshock
ISBN: 978-1-937551-26-1

Earn Bonus Bucks!

Earn 1 Bonus Buck for each dollar you spend. Find out how at
RiptidePublishing.com/news/bonus-bucks.

Win Free Ebooks for a Year!

Pre-order coming soon titles directly through our site and you'll receive
one entry into a drawing to win free books for a year! Get the details at
RiptidePublishing.com/contests.

Lightning Source UK Ltd.
Milton Keynes UK
UKOW042322240313

208071UK00024B/71/P